Host a Little Ghost and the Story of the Mystical Mums

By Coauthors:
Kevin McCormick
Lillian Stulich
Illustrations by Bill Dishon

"Dedicated to Our Families."

HOST A LITTLE GHOST and the Story of the Mystical Mums

Little Ghost Publishing
www.littleghostpublishing.com

Paperback ISBN: 978-0-578-14403-0
Hardback ISBN: 978-0-578-14415-3

The Myth of the Halloween Mums.

Magical, mystical fall flowers...

Usually attract Halloween spirits with fragrant, charming powers...

Many children believe this to be true...

So read this story, and you might, too!

A plain-round pumpkin was transformed into a smiling jack-o-lantern on
a crisp fall day. The twins, Tommy and Suzie, loved this time of year...Autumn.
They placed "Jack" on the front porch,
put on light-weight jackets and went over to the big old tree.
Suzie carried two spades and Tommy carried a box of colorful mums.

They had heard about the myth of the mystical mums
and wanted desperately to find out if it was true.
If they planted the mums, would they be lucky enough
to hear or see the Halloween spirits?
They hoped, they wished, but most of all, they planted.....

Just as they finished planting the last fragrant mum, an autumn wind
started to blow. The children watched in wonder as a whirlwind swirled
the colorful leaves up around the big old tree. They stared... mesmerized...
for they had never seen such a sight! Could this be part of the Halloween tale?
They did not see, but hidden in the whirlwind of rustling leaves was
a little ghost who was lifted high onto a branch in the big old tree.

The twins' thoughts were interrupted by their mother's voice calling them for lunch.
They raced each other down the path that led to the front porch
and waved to "Jack" as they went into the house.
Little did the twins know that following them was a new friend!

During lunch Tommy and Suzie were telling Mommy what they had seen.
Their mother could not believe it!
She had heard of the myth of the mystical mums when she was around their age, too.
She wondered could the myth actually be true?!?

As the twins continued to tell Mommy what they saw,
she went to the pantry and opened the door.
The light bulb began to flicker...
The fragrance of mums drifted past her.
There, on the shelf sat a glowing little ghost.
Mommy let out a gasp!
The little ghost let out a "shush!"

Then in a whispering voice the little ghost said,

"I was playing among the mums; listening to the words spoken by your little ones...

Suddenly a fall gust of wind sent me whirling up to a branch in the big old tree.

From high up on the branch I could see, your home might be a nice place for me.

I am a little ghost, looking for a loving host.

The myth of the mums is true...

I know that you believe this, too!

Halloween is when ghosts roam, looking for a loving home.

I will watch Tommy and Suzie for the next thirteen days.

If they are good children I just might stay.

When I see them listen to you, a treat they will receive.

But if they do not listen to you, a note I will leave.

Here are three rules you can tell them I said:

*Play nicely with one another and learn to share.

*Be responsible with their care.

*Love each other, be a good sister and brother."

Quickly Mommy turned and called,
"Tommy, Suzie, come here and see!
There is a little ghost in our pantry!"
But when the children ran to see the sight,
All they saw was a flickering light.
"Where did the little ghost go?" they said.
All Mommy could do was shake her head.
Mommy said, "Tommy and Suzie don't frown.
Let us have a look around."
They looked and looked but as hard as they did,
They could not find where the little ghost hid!

So Mommy told the twins about the three rules and the treats that they might find.

If they listen to Mommy, were well behaved, and kind.

For thirteen days before Halloween night, the little ghost might appear in sight.

Mommy then asked the twins if they understood.

Tommy and Suzie nodded their heads yes, and said, "We'll be good."

That night the children put their pajamas on, brushed their teeth and quickly went to bed.

Dreams about Halloween mums and ghosts filled the little ones' heads.

The sun's morning rays woke the twins from their dreams.

It was now thirteen days until Halloween!

After making their beds they went down the stairs...

Into the kitchen, they pulled out their chairs.

There sitting in Suzie's seat was the little ghost with the twins' first treat.

Mommy turned and looked surprised, and had a twinkle in her eyes.

She knew that Tommy and Suzie would love their new friend,

Who would teach them the three rules in the end!

Tommy and Suzie put their plates in the sink, then went outside to play.

They took along the little ghost that they had met that day!

The thirteen days till Halloween did not last.
The blustery days of fall went by fast!
Halloween was getting near,
Each night the little ghost would disappear.
When morning came Tommy and Suzie would search around,
Until the little ghost was found.
It was great fun to find where the little ghost would hide,
For there was always a treat by the little ghost's side!

The children forgot to brush their teeth one night.
The next day the little ghost had left a note, and no treat was in sight!
The note read, "Brush your teeth every day. If you want me,
The little ghost, to come out and play."

Tommy and Suzie knew the little ghost liked to play
And hide some place all through the day.
If they were good and looked around,
The little ghost could be found.
With treats and goodies that are nice,
And, yes, a note, left once or twice.

Today was Halloween!

Tommy and Suzie looked all through the day...

Their little ghost friend must have gone away...

The children were sad, their new friend they missed.

Tommy and Suzie learned many lessons from the little ghost's list!

Costume time was getting near...

The twins changed into their pirate gear.

Mommy walked with Tommy and Suzie to Trick or Treat.
And from all the smiling neighbors they did meet;
The children had their bags filled with goodies to eat!

Heading back home with bags full; almost.

The twins never stopped thinking about the little ghost.

As they entered the yard by the big old tree, where they would often play;
Was the greatest treat they would receive, on this Halloween day!
There glowing brightly beside the mystical mums,
The little ghost had returned to the place where the story had begun.

Tommy and Suzie adopted the ghost,
Who was happy to have more than just a host.
The little ghost who once sat high on a branch of a big old tree,
Was now was part of a loving family.

The End.

Ghost Script:
If you listen to your parents and are kind,
A little ghost you might find,
Who will leave some treats until Halloween day,
And in the end, your own little ghost will stay!

*What is the special place where Mommy will let you leave your little ghost at night?
Make sure it is alright with Mommy.

Tommy and Suzie chose the dresser where the little ghost would sit each night.
But, when morning came the little ghost was nowhere in sight.
The little ghost seemed to magically reappear in the many places listed here:

On the children's chair.
In the pantry.
Under the bed.
On the sunny window ledge.
By the mailbox.

Here is a list of some treats the little ghost left for the twins:

A special candy treat or a little Halloween toy.
Halloween sprinkles, for cupcakes Mommy baked.
A Halloween eraser and pencil.
A little flashlight to carry for Trick or Treating.
A Trick or Treat bag or container.
Decorations for Halloween.

The "Ghost It Notes" left by the little ghost reminded the twins to:

Brush their teeth every day.
Put their plates in the sink.
Put their toys away.
Share when they play.

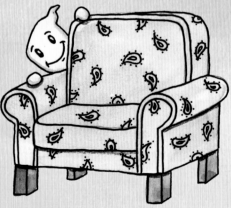

(For your own little ghost who might travel to you in an October whirlwind.)

I was attracted by the mystical mums planted by the tree,
And the sounds of loving children playing happily.
I traveled on a whirlwind and came to be with you.
So now it's time to adopt me and here is what you do.
With the help of a loving person, please fill in below.
The blanks are where your name and my new name will go.
I will be with you forever as part of your happy family.
I am no longer the little ghost sitting in the tree.

_____

Your Name

_____

Your Little Ghost's Name